PACIFIC

NORTHWEST

JASON MERRILL

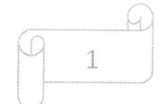

Pacific North West

Pacific North West

Pacific North West

I was asked if I could sum up the experience of life in one word; I simply smiled and spoke not a word. The question seemed to be at best boring and mundane. How to some up love, fear, hate, power, loss, gain, amongst others in one word? My tragedies would make me into a wanderer, that wandering would turn me into a believer.

The loss of something or someone important can turn a simple meandering way of life into a downward spiral, or into a rocket ship hurling itself out of control. For me I guess this was a little bit of both. Would the ride that felt so damning turn itself into something I wouldn't want to see the end of? I had no idea that life could produce such beautiful petals on such an evil stem.

The color *palette* of my life would be painted *with* the darkest of colors, *glistening* in the sun on the outside, but *darkening* even the brightest of places inside. Well, that was until I met her, an angel faced beauty with a soul so full of fire no ocean could put her out. After meeting her I would never feel the same about the path I walked, let alone about the way I perceived the world.

In the middle of a forest fire called life, bloomed an angel that was meant for me... or was she? I thought I had it all figured out until I met her, the flower that could have saved me from my own destruction.

Pacific North West

Pacific North West

PACIFIC

NORTHWEST

JASON MERRILL

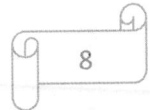

Pacific North West

To Aria Merrill

May the world leave

You amazed by

Its beauty.

For Amanda

With love.

Pacific North West

Thank you

Sharon Debidour

You've made this work

Not just a hobby,

But a way of life!

Pacific North West

The dreams that live are

Only realized

If you live them.

— Jason Merrill

Pacific North West

Thank you

Nik Clark

For your

Artistic abilities.

Pacific North West

Caelah Clark

You inspire me beyond the sunset.

CHAPTERS

1. Gridlock
2. Possibilities
3. Peace
4. Middle of Nowhere
5. Questions
6. Backdrops
7. A Hurtful Reminder
8. Nightmares
9. Home
10. Life

Pacific North West

Pacific North West

Pacific North West

Chapter One

GRIDLOCK

Pacific North West

The sound of gridlock and people in a hurry with nowhere of real importance to go was the norm around here. Don't get me wrong I love the sound of the city, and the blinding lights. Well at least I used to. My days primarily start off the same as everyone else's; I wake up, I walk to work, punch the clock, repeat day in and day out. Is this what life's about, or have we all worked ourselves into a life we really could not care less about?

At least one thing was looking up; spring was on the horizon which made the winter frost more and more tolerable. Not that I minded winter, or at least I didn't until the last couple of years that have been so taxing. Well here I am early on a Monday morning punching a card that in my mind symbolized the punching of hours away from my life. My time card, that time clock clicked as if it were laughing. Then again it did consume most of my existence.

"Jackson, you're late by two minutes. One more time and that's a write up, guy!"

My boss Howard Wrenshaw, a real piece of work, was as always greeting his employees with the respect that they deserved. "I'm sorry Mr. Wrenshaw, it won't happen again." Besides if it did I was more than over this job and this place.

"I hope not, I see this winter has taken a real toll on you, you look like a beat dog, and if you're beaten down at the start of spring, well then you're not much use to me. Get to work!"

The sounds of pounding machinery, beating like a drum, methodically over and over, and all you can do to escape the pounding is to try and ignore it. In this place heat poured out of every crack in every piece of equipment. People far less enthusiastic about their job than myself, filled this dusty, dirty hole that consumed most of our conscious life. To put it mildly I needed a break before I was broken down completely.

All day I welded steel together. Nothing fancy but it paid the bills. All day long I waited patiently for a bell just loud enough to hear over the relentless sound of metal on metal, signaling I could escape this cave, the day was over, and enjoy the peace of city life on my walk home.

Every day the same, but somehow different all at once. A million-different people doing *essentially* the same thing with small and subtle differences from one to the other. Street entertainment is something everyone should see at least once in their life. Come on, where else would you see a man juggle just steps away from a half nude man playing a guitar? I mean if they were to team up they would have an impressive act.

Did I mention they performed just steps from the front entrance to the building in which I lived?

Nothing better than pushing the front door open, signaling the end of another day.

The squeaky old door was a sound for sore ears, letting me know just a few steps to climb, picking up a few neighborly conversations through the thin walls, until finally, I'm home.

A small studio apartment in the middle of the city, two windows a door, and a bed was my rented world. The bed wasn't entirely necessary, as I barely slept, sleep haunted by screams, screams I was powerless to help.

At night, I would sit at the foot of my bed listening to the sounds of nature downloaded onto my phone. Peace and tranquility was my attempt to ease the burden of what had become my life. With my modest living I had managed to save enough money to buy a small van that sat waiting for me to drive it anywhere, and set aside a little extra in my savings for a rainy day. Honestly, I'm not sure why I spent the money on the van. I only drive it once a month to get to the park up state to hike for the weekend.

Being outdoors brings me peace, a feeling of something greater than myself staring me in the face, a landscape so perfect that had yet to be spoiled by the touch of man.

With the extra money I've been fortunate enough to save over last two years, I had high hopes of buying a small house north of the city. I had studied Forestry and dreamed of landing a job up state in the forestry department, working in the field I loved with a passion, and being free from the city. Well, that thought alone was more than I needed on the difficult days to pull myself through them.

As if the nights weren't difficult enough to sleep through without any further distractions, I could hear my neighbor next door crying every night on the phone, simply trying to borrow money from whom ever she would call just to make ends meet. She lived there with her new born baby - she was so proud of her little girl. When we would pass in the hall I knew she smiled because she had something to be proud of. I heard from the landlord Kenny Walsh, an all-around good guy and one of my only friends, that her husband and father of the little girl, was killed in a car accident days before the baby was born, a tragedy that struck all too close to home. My heart broke for her.

Pacific North West

Tragedy seemingly surrounded me like a magnetic force, pulling heartbreak to me. I wanted to change this and help people, but lacked the gusto most days. Then again if we all helped one another out a little more often than never, the world would shine a little brighter.

Don't get me wrong, some mornings were better than others. The relentless snow and piles of ice began to give way to paths beaten through them by the busy travelers of the nights and days. The smell of the café on the corner was one of my favorite things on the way to work, although I had never stopped in. My modest life was what had afforded me my van and my soon to be home upstate, away from all the stress that had become my life.

Day in and day out the sound of humans filled the air, each busier than the next, screaming and yelling, honking and cursing their way to and from work, or wherever was so important that humanity escaped most of them altogether.

Not sure if I was just a sideline quarterback, or that I didn't have the time, but I never stepped into anyone else's business if they steered clear of mine. It wasn't worth fighting for someone that had no fight left in them. I didn't want to add to a world of carnage. I wanted to escape it.

This week I had planned to start work at noon on Monday, as I needed time at the bank to start the application process to buy my new get away place up north. Not too long after sitting down I started to realize something. While I sat in that less than comfortable "fancy" chair, watching all the long faces waiting in longer than necessary lines, due to lack of workers, I realized that no one at all looked happy, not even remotely. Surely if this is a place that holds all your money, shouldn't you be smiling when coming and going from it?

Instead as I overheard people begging for extensions, and trying to explain why they needed a fee reversed I had an epiphany, and with that realization I stood up, walked over to the nearest desk, sitting down across from the banker.

"I would like to withdraw all of my money, and close my accounts please."

"Absolutely Sir, may I ask is there any reason in particular why you are leaving our bank? Is there anything I could do to keep you as a customer?"

I sat for a moment "Actually, yes. I'm going to enjoy my life and no longer be chained by the reality that has been okayed by the everyday Joe. As far as keeping me as a customer, no thank you. I would just as soon be treated like a person, not a customer. But thank you for asking!"

With a look of shock upon her face, she took my withdrawal slip with her and disappeared behind the counter.

I sat patiently waiting for about thirty minutes when she resurfaced with a man, carrying a banking bag in his left hand.

"Well, Sir, here is your money if you could step this way with me. Due to the size of the transaction I must have the money counted in front of both of us for us both to sign off on the transaction."

I followed behind the man to a private room where my cash was run through a machine. With every bill that clicked through that machine freedom clicked closer and closer.

"There you are Sir, One Hundred Twenty-Two Thousand Forty-One dollars and Fifty-Seven cents."

 Signing my name on that line, looking at a lifetime of savings in a couple of bags, I felt a small sense of freedom, a feeling of life returning to me. I placed the money into my hiking pack and continued my way to work, business as usual.

The air felt a bit warmer on my walk that day. I wasn't at all sure what I was going to do with the money or myself for that matter. I knew one thing though. I refused to be tied down by bills, and a job I hated since my first day on the floor. Even if it meant taking the money out of the bank just to put it back in, to feel free for a little while, so be it.

Along my walk, I stopped and gazed out over the bay, watching the water, listening to the peace that was offered by the depth of it. I had a smile on my face for the first time in a very long time.

My walk concluded with me standing in front of the factory entrance where I worked. My smile had been wiped away, replaced with a blank slate and an empty feeling. This building and its contents were one of the main reasons my life was so unhappy. But I needed this place to survive, or at least I thought I did.

I pulled open the door entering the noise filled filth for what seemed like the millionth time.

I wasn't sure of too many people's names at work; probably because I hadn't cared to learn them. I never planned on being here this long, and surely not much longer. I usually didn't concern myself with any of the goings on, only my job for the most part. I didn't need to know what anyone had done last night or was doing after work, although for some reason today was different. As I walked past the front office a young lady emerged crying and visibly shaken up.

"What's the matter?" I asked her. As she began to open her mouth, not only could I hear his loud mouth open, I could feel his hot breath on my neck. He began to yell.

"It's none of your damn business what's wrong with her. Now get to work before I make you cry next!"

Without thinking, I turned, striking Mr. Wrenshaw right in his mouth, knocking him to the floor, bleeding from the corner of his mouth. I stood over top of him enraged.

"I'm so sick of you yelling at the people that make you "Your Money" that I want to break you in half. You have yelled at me for the last time, you punk piece of garbage. I quit! If you have anything to say, say it now, tough guy, not when I walk out that door."

Silence fell over the factory as every employee for the first time that I knew of had smiles upon their faces. With one last look at Mr. Wrenshaw I smiled. "Good luck with this dump, you ungrateful sack."

The almost spring sun warmed my face. I walked out of that factory door for the last time. I felt free, freer than I have in a long time. Now life could begin again. Now life could begin to heal me.

~

Invigorated, so many thoughts running through my head, I was home in no time at all. I began to pack up my clothes and the belongings that held a special place in my heart. I put my wooden beaded necklace on for the first time in two years, and carried three bags and two boxes out to my van.

I re-entered the building for a final glance over to make sure I hadn't left anything that mattered to me behind. Nothing but the bigger furniture, television and a rug sat waiting for the next tenant. With one last flip of the switch, out went the lights. I turned the key and locked the door behind me.

A muffled cry had caught my ear as I walked past my neighbor's door., I could hear her talking on the phone.

"Dad, please, I start my new job on Monday and Shirley from down the hall is going to watch the baby for free until I can afford to pay her. Please help me... I know this is my mess. Do you think I wanted him to die?

My life is a disaster and I'm doing my best to get back on track..."

The conversation continued, but I had heard enough. This life puzzles me more and more each day. How could you turn your back on your own family, especially when the circumstances such as hers were so terrible?

A few stops to go before I left the building. I dug into my pack, pulling out four thousand dollars and knocked on Shirley's door.

"Hello Shirley. We've never really talked but my name is Jackson. I live - well I lived - down the hall...Anyways I'm moving out today and wanted to stop by and pay my neighbor Maria's babysitting fee in advance for her. Here is four thousand dollars to cover for a little while."

Shirley smiled. She knew that Maria had no idea of what I was up too. "I always knew there was something special about you, young man. I could just tell from the feeling I would get when I passed you in the hall, or the lobby. May you be blessed in your travels, wherever they may take you."

I smiled. "Thank you."

Only one more stop to make as I entered the landlord's office and handed him my keys. "Mr. Jones, I would like to pay the rent of Maria in three zero four."

Mr. Jones looked up from his paperwork. "My boy I have been helping her as well for a few months now. She's already three months behind. I know the circumstances, so I would never throw her out. I know she'll get back on her feet."

I paused for a moment. That was one of the things I would miss about this building and the people in it; their willingness to help one another with little or nothing expected in return. They say that's what truly makes one great - helping someone that could never repay you. I dug into my pack.

"Well at seven hundred a month times three, that's twenty-one hundred. Now twelve times seven that's eighty-four hundred, so ten thousand five hundred will pay her up for the next year."

I pulled the money from my pack and handed it to Mr. Jones. He smiled from ear to ear and began to count the money.

"Here Jackson, take this back."

He handed back to me half of the money. "I'll tell you what. I'll split the year and the past due with you."

I stood from my seat, shook Mr. Jones hand and walked out the door of the place I had called home with a smile on my face. The sound of silence as I started the van, now with only one more stop to make before I headed out of town.

~

My final stop was at the local cemetery to pay a visit to someone whom I'd lost a couple of years back, I sat next to her grave and felt all the pain and emotions resonate immediately to the surface.

"Well, my love, this isn't good bye, but it is bye for now. I'm so sorry I just couldn't stay here anymore. I will always carry you with me, and I will always love you. Until I see you again, you will be with me in all that I do."

I held my beaded necklace tight while tears rolled down my face. I wiped my face and walked away from one of the anchors in my life. I could barely move after she had left, and it still all but paralyzes me to come back here.

Not real sure of where I was heading and not wanting to settle down in that house up state just yet I noticed and pulled a flyer from under my wiper. "Come see the "Pacific North West" play tonight. With that taken as a sign from above, my journey west began.

Chapter Two

POSSIBILITIES

With so much to see and so many possibilities, the thought of my journey made me jittery, so much so that I felt for the first time in a long time that I actually wanted to remember my journey. I had a feeling that memories to come would be happy, not days on end that I wished away. One of the saddest parts of life is that most people wish their lives away to get to a day off, or to make it to the weekend. With that kind of life is anyone really living?

I pulled the van over about thirty minutes outside of downtown, stopping in front of a camera shop. The shop owner was more than helpful with my purchase. I let him know I needed something easy to use in rough climates. After talking for about a half hour I purchased the best camera and lens that I could figure out how to use on the fly. With a piece of equipment that could keep a photographic log of my new life, the journey could now really begin.

Pacific North West

My head swirled. I figured that the best plan of action would be to look over a map and have a decent meal, one last Coney dog and a plate of fries, while looking at all the possibilities that lay ahead of me.

As I left New York heading West with so many possible destinations laying in front of me my excitement grew. My journey would take me roughly two thousand nine hundred and forty-nine miles west, and from there south into Oregon. I would pass through Pennsylvania, Ohio, Indiana, Illinois, Wisconsin, Minnesota, North Dakota, Montana, Idaho, Washington, finishing in Oregon.

Without very much in the way of life experience that hadn't been terrible or traumatic I was hungry for anything, and everything. Tires humming against the interstate, windows partially down for fresh air, I could see my first big state line sign on the horizon.

"Welcome to Pennsylvania", I read the sign aloud. I was more than looking forward to taking photos and enjoying the 2400 square miles of the Pocono Mountains, which spanned Carbon, Monroe, Pike, and Wayne counties. The first thing that captured my eye was a high ropes and zip line park. I had to stop.

Flying through the air with the ability to just let go, I was more than ready. I figured this would help me let go. Maybe my new travels would help me just let go?

"Hello sir, how may I help you?" asked a friendly young man behind the counter.

"I would like to try zip lining."

"Absolutely sir, it'll be forty-nine dollars for the day or thirty-five dollars for half the day."

For that price, I wasn't leaving until the sun went down. "I'll take the day pass, please!"

With my gear strapped on and a fifteen-minute instructional, I was ready to climb high in the trees and zip back to earth like a bird. The wind in my face, cruising across what seemed like miles of steel cable, took my breath away.

Tears from wind not sadness, or everyday life made me realize that I had been my own worst enemy in this thing called life. I guess the old saying is true; If you get knocked down, get back up again. She would've been so very disappointed in the way I had let life escape me for so long.

A beautiful sunset over the mountains signaled it was time for me to get some sleep. A local camp ground offered a nice spot to park the van and sleep inside for the night. I hadn't planned this whole trip very well, as I was lacking the basic camping gear to survive a night in the woods.

Who would have ever thought that a van would make such a nice comfortable place to sleep? I really should've been sleeping in here, saving money, instead of all the money spent living in that little apartment. I had a relatively sleepless night. Not sure if it was the jitters, or the simple fact that I had no idea what I was doing?

As the sun rose over the trees, I was already snapping photos of the local wildlife, and endless backdrops. Waterfalls, woodlands, and rivers made my choice to leave this place very difficult. But I knew that I had a plan laid out and wanted to stick to it. Besides - how would I know where I wanted to end up if I didn't see it all?

One more stop at Curwensville Lake, A quick adjustment of the heat in the van to max and I was off. I jumped into the chilly water for a quick swim and a quick cleanup. After dressing in the van I sat watching fishermen with their kids; this brought back memories.

"As a child, I rarely received love from anyone. I was an only child and my mother passed away when I was only two. My father worked enough to keep a roof over our heads and food on the table. After mom passed he all but gave up on life. I had always believed that the reason he had never showed me affection or love was because he didn't want to be close to anyone ever again.

My father wasted away, drinking most of the time that he had free, and when he was sober he couldn't even look at me half of the time. I knew somehow it was because I looked too much like my mother.

I had always believed that he loved me, keeping my hope of feeling love alive. Shortly after I turned eighteen my father died of a heart attack in his sleep. Well at least that was the medical term. I believe he wanted me to make it to that age, so I couldn't be put in a home, and then he died of a broken heart.

Delaying his death until I was old enough to be on my own was the only way he ever showed me that that he loved me. After watching him punish himself through life, I swore I would never let that happen to me.

~

Pacific North West

With all my fond childhood memories fresh again, it was time to get back on the road. Interstate I-80 stretched out before me. As far as I could see trees and massive rocks were dug out, clearing the way to make room for modern man's travels. I would like to say my mind raced with possibilities, but it didn't for once - it was clear. I couldn't even begin to imagine what lie in front of me. I wasn't sure if I was looking for anything in particular or just running from something that pained me.

My mind began to clutter with nonsense again. Luckily a distraction appeared in the form of a sign for Cedar Pointe. I had heard of this iron jungle many times but never had the opportunity to visit.

~

For a nominal fee and a distant hike across the asphalt parking lot, I was ready to ride some of the most intense rides in the country.

I stood in line for hours for rides that would last barely a few minutes, some less than that. Well worth the wait. I had read so much about this place and scrutinized the map contemplating a day filled with adrenaline.

Once I had my fill of rides, racing up and down, twisting and turning, I feasted on great old American food. I am the biggest sucker for corn dogs and elephant ears. There were few places back home offering such fine cuisine. I tried my hand at a slew of carnival games, winning a bunch of stuffed animals I had absolutely no use for. I was then ready to play some old-fashioned arcade games. One of my great childhood escapes from everyday life was an old run down arcade a few blocks from where I grew up. A Friday night spent searching for loose change usually lead to a Saturday away from the empty house.

After a day full of sun drenched adrenaline I was more than ready to take a short break at one of the rest stops along the way.

That night I tossed and turned a little more than the previous night, uncertain if my restlessness was caused by knowing there was no turning back at this point, or that there was nowhere to turn back to. Nonetheless my new life was in front of me and there was nothing stopping me anymore. If I felt alone and as if I had failed now, it would be of my own accord, no one else's.

~

That next morning, I laughing quietly to myself as I watched the sleep deprived men slapping their faces, showering their heads under a sink faucet, and purchasing every energy drink in the vending machines. The difference for me was I was in no hurry and had no real end point in mind. I was free, the kind of freedom that so many dream of, with that realization I would enjoy every minute of this journey.

Brushed my teeth, and then picked up a coffee and a donut, that were more than overpriced, but in these places, you had to pay the piper. Now I was ready for a day of straight through driving in Indiana.

Pacific North West

I may have picked a bad day not to take a break in the early going - figures my mind would get the better of me. From the back of my mind crept forward a memory I cannot erase.

Her face was like porcelain, her hair swept across her with such shine; her smile could light up an abyss, eyes that glimmered like stars, and a heart that was bigger than the Grand Canyon.

She kept me safe, she kept me alive and she loved me unconditionally. My flaws ceased to exist and my failures never happened. She kept me from being hurt, and made me feel full of love and life.

The day she left this place I reverted to that time when I felt alone and unloved, giving me more reason to aim to treat every person, regardless of stature, with kindness and respect.

I realized that no matter what is going on in my life, no one knew the battles I faced, just as I had no idea what battle any other soul was fighting.

On a good day, she wouldn't cross my mind more than a hundred times or so, on a bad day I wasn't sure how I would make it through the day.

I asked myself the same question all the time. Would I ever allow myself to love again, and would it even be possible?

~

On the best of days, we often talked about our dreams for our future.

"Why don't we just go? If we leave this weekend we could find new jobs, and our new home. After that we rest and enjoy life as we like."

I looked at her. Her long auburn hair swept across her face almost enough to cover her emerald green eyes, with such a delicate face I often wondered if she were an angel.

"Hannah, you make my heart smile! I want nothing more than to leave this busy rat race of city life, but we need to have just a little more in savings. I'd say at most another six months and we're out of here."

She knew I would stretch the six months into eight; I wanted to buy our home outright, so we didn't have a mortgage hanging over us every day for the next fifteen to thirty years like a jail sentence.

"I think four to six months would be more in the ballpark. Besides if we look in the right areas, we'll have no trouble finding a nice place in our budget," she replied hopefully.

Every night I sat and stared out into the unending lights of the big city knowing she was right; we should just pack up and go. I'm not sure what the hang up was for me; maybe thinking about how we used to struggle to buy groceries to make it through a few days. Or maybe that I liked having new socks occasionally. For us to just up and go meant leaving behind jobs that neither of us was too fond of, but they paid us well enough.

Sitting looking out over the night I realized how great our lives together were. I finally had gotten up the courage to buy a ring and had a surprise planned on our next upstate hike, which was only a day away.

~

She was on to me, maybe not on the exact path, but she knew I was up to something.

"You've been extremely quiet on the drive up. Is something the matter?"

I was trying to play it cool.

"No…No, I have a lot on my mind after this week at work, besides you're not saying a whole lot either." I said, deflecting the attention away from me.

"Ok, if you say so. I hope there will be more conversation and less thinking about that trap of life back home when we get to the trails," she sighed.

She knew if my behavior was off even in the slightest of degree. She was absolutely perfect in every way. Being with her made me feel worthy and so fortunate just to hold her when she awakens in the morning, and as she dozes off to sleep at night. Knowing she loved me unconditionally was the most amazing feeling in my life.

"We're here. I know you wanted a peaceful weekend, so instead of hitting the trails and tenting at night I took the liberty of renting us a cabin in the hiking village."

She paused for a moment not giving any indication if this was a wise move or not on my part.

"I think you made a wonderful decision, plus we don't have to haul everything with us when we hike out now, so we can go further in a day without wearing down so quickly."
We walked to the front door of a small one room cabin that had room enough for a pullout sleeper, a wood burning stove in the corner, and a small table and chairs to eat at. Little did she know I had a surprise waiting when we pushed the door open.

She walked in slowly, looking around in amazement. I had roses placed throughout the cabin, candles lit upon the table and her favorite song playing in the background. I waited on one knee in the doorway of the cabin for her to turn around, a ring

symbolizing her beauty and my love in hand. She turned.
I will remember forever the look of astonishment on her face and the joy that radiated from her.

"Hannah Hatcher, will you make me the happiest man in the world and do me the honor of marrying me?"

"Yes…Yes oh my gosh, yes. How did you do all of this? I knew you were being too quiet on the ride up here."
Before she could say another word I took her by the hand slipped the ring on and kissed her.

"I took a day off of work last week ,came up here, and had Jim at the front office help me out. I shot him a text from the store just down the road from here and he ran over to light the candles and put out the flowers, turn on the music."

She smiled radiantly as she jumped on my back. I carried her all around the campsite and back to the door of the cabin, as she talked to me like we've done so many times before.

"I cannot believe that you did all of this. I mean this is absolutely unreal. I would have never in a million years guessed this is what you were up too. I can't believe you kept this a secret! You can't keep anything secret from me."

I laughed.

"That's why I shop for you the night before your birthday. But this time I knew I had to keep it as quiet as possible. I wanted to see the smile that only you are capable of smiling. I love you with all of my heart, Hannah Hatcher."

"I love you too Jackson, always and forever."

That night the stars burned brighter, and the moon lit up the interior of the cabin walls. We lay hopelessly entangled within one another, nothing but the night between us. Nights such as these made the entire journey through this life well worth it.

~

My least favorite part of the weekends was packing up and leaving. We traveled upstate often the entire our entire time together.

The way we figured it life consisted of two parts; ours and theirs. Theirs was the time we spent commuting to and from work and the time spent at work to pay for a lot of unnecessary things in life that were really nothing more than time wasters.

Then there was the ours. Ours was the time in between the rigorous demands of life. Sleeping, talking, playing, hiking and just spending time together doing what we wanted to do, whether conquering the world, or just lying in a hammock together. We loved our time together.

"I'm going to miss this place."

She laughed at me. "You say that every time we leave here. You know we'll be back again - we always find our way back here. It's kind of who we are."

I loved that she had a way of putting things into perspective in a way that I could relate to.
She usually slept on the way home, which gave me time to think about life and the direction the road had taken me.

Without much in the way of a home life before I met her, I wasn't sure what I did without her.

We did everything together and I couldn't wait to marry her and spend the rest of our lives together.

"Jackson don't forget I have a meeting after work tonight. I love you - see you later." She hugged and kissed me as she went out the door to work.

I pushed my way through the work day and made my way home. I sat waiting for her call to let me know she was on her way home, when the phone rang.

"Hello, is this Jackson Mathew?"

"Yes, it is. May I ask whose calling?"

"Sir, this is Doctor Grady from BI County Hospital. You are listed as the primary contact for Hanna Hatcher. Would this be correct?"

My heart began to sink. "Yes...Yes that is correct."

"Sir, she's been in an accident."

"How? She doesn't drive - is she ok? Is she alive?"

I waited and the pause seemed to last forever before he responded.

"I'm so sorry sir, your Miss. Hatcher was pronounced dead at the scene. She was hit by a car crossing Fifth Street."

I dropped the phone to floor barely listening to him say I could come down and identify her body. I walked to the hospital in disbelief, knowing my world had just come to an end; knowing she would have been home; she would have answered her phone by now.
I was taken back through a series of corridors and hallways with a smell I'll never forget. They led me into a room and uncovered her; she was cold and stained with blood. I had seen enough. Tears rolled freely down my face.

Pacific North West

Over the next couple of days, I would arrange to have her buried, and with no family on either side, I stood and watched as she was laid to rest.

I stood for what had to be hours looking at the fresh dirt that now lay over her grave. With nothing left to live for my life had just become a much darker place.

Over the Horizon I could see Illinois racing in my direction, smiling as I drove toward the big city, and oddly comforted by the impressive skyline of Chicago skyscrapers.

I had a short list of things to see and do while in the city. First stop was the Field museum. I wanted to wander the halls of that place forever. So many places to travel within the walls of that single building.

I enjoy that people treat museums like the library, speaking quietly as if the exhibits are listening. On display were the infamous man-eating lions, two of whom were made famous by Hollywood, and although the other had a less interesting story he killed more men all on his own.

~

Pacific North West

After a couple of hours strolling through the Art Institute of Chicago I made my way to the Shedds Aquarium, a place where I could be under water without getting wet.

I must tell you coming face to face with a green sea turtle was one of the most amazing things I have ever done. The look of peace in that animal's eye, almost like he knew what I had hidden behind mine was completely unreal.

~

I had yet another stop on my list before I could get some rest, the Adler Planetarium. I purchased my tickets and reclined back in my seat, watching the panoramic night sky roll across the ceiling. I was happy and saddened by this place all at the same time.

The ability to see the solar system and the stars was completely amazing, but on the other hand this place would be the only place that most of the local people would ever see this in their entire lives.

Not that every night of mine was filled with star studded skies, but when I could and would escape north, the views were amazing, and the night skies breathtaking.

My day here finished up with a stay at the Millennium Knickerbocker Hotel, a place unlike any other. I stayed on a floor as high as I could to remember the view of where I had left, and to look forward to what lay ahead.

CHAPTER THREE

PEACE

Waking up to the sounds of the city streets and noise of the passersby, I quickly remembered why I had begun this journey, "Peace".

Street side coffee and bagel in hand, I was ready to continue my voyage. Rolling along with the spring sun warm on my arm, resting in the window, I sensed the weather had finally broken and spring had sprung.

From the moment I started my drive westward I knew one of the places that I had to stop and see was "Nickelodeon Universe" in Bloomington, Minnesota. Call it the kid in me, but I had forever wanted to visit that place.

Finally, I saw the mall in the background. The size of the place was amazing. How could so many places, in one location, stay in business? But what do I know about business? I quit my job, withdrew my life savings, and headed across country to find something with no idea of what it even is.

When I first entered the indoor amusement park I had waited so long to see, I was smiling ear to ear as if I were a small boy. That joy was suddenly replaced as I stood in line to pay for my new t-shirt with sorrow.

I walked back to the van, trying to figure out who was wrong - me or my father?

Driving away with a strong wind rushing through the open windows, I watched the scenery pass, deep in thought.

How could my father have never taken me to a place I wanted to see so badly as a child? Or am I to blame that I had never asked him after the initial time? Nonetheless he should have taken me, taken us, anywhere. I mean it may have done us both some good to be away from our home, the shrine of my dead mother.

How was one to heal with constant reminders of her?

~

Absorbed in the beauty of North Dakota, the drive thru this vast and heavy terrain had gone by so fast, I couldn't believe I had all but reached Montana.

I could tell that the dark would soon fall around me, and I knew I wanted to see the "Northern Lights" from Lolo National Forest.

I had read about the forest, rivers, and the night sky in so many books and magazines. With high hopes of putting my new camera to use, I arrived at the park.

"Hello. What type of pass can I help you with?" the young lady from the ticket booth asked politely.

"I would like a campsite please. Would you happen to know a spot where I could take some photographs of the Northern Lights?"

"I have a bluff spot about a mile or so in, that is available. I can show you the way back if you'd like."

I could feel the excitement building; I was going to see the Northern Lights. "That would be perfect, thank you!"

She made her way to a four wheel off road park vehicle, and then motioned for me to follow her. After about three minutes or so she turned around pointed to the spot, and waved goodbye.

I couldn't park the van fast enough and run to the edge of the bluff. I felt the wind taken from my lungs; words couldn't paint a picture of the emotion and feeling of life that rushed through my veins as I looked out over the beauty of that scene not been touched by man, since the beginning of time.

~

Tonight I wanted to be one with nature. I rolled out my hammock and strapped it between two trees. I jumped up into it giving it the weight test, swinging a bit. This will do perfectly.

Nightfall couldn't come fast enough. I waited as a small child waiting for Christmas morning. The moon moved into place, the stars beginning to give away their hiding places, and the sky lit up more beautifully than any sky I had ever seen. My body warmed with a feeling of awe, I was humbled to be so small in what felt like such a magical place.

My camera sat at the ready on its tri-pod waiting for me to snap away. When a flash of light appeared, green then purple, followed by blues and more greens and purples.

My finger held the auto shoot button down snapping photo after photo, and me smiling from ear to ear. Yet somewhere in that moment, in all that happiness, I thought of her, how she would have loved this entire trip, and how much moments like this made me miss her.

Moments like this made me feel bad for my father, and made me realize that for him it was easier to stay put in the house, rather than feel guilty about being happy.

I continued taking pictures until the first sim card was full, not realizing it was four o'clock in the morning.

I had to try and sleep through all this amazement, or I would never make it through Idaho tomorrow.

~

Fresh crisp morning air blew across the hammock, rattling the straps. As quick as I could I rolled out of my sleeping bag and leapt to the ground to greet the spring air.

Still a bit chilly this time of year, which I didn't mind at all, the clean mountain air filled my lungs, and I couldn't believe how one could feel so alive in the middle of nowhere, all alone.

While packing up my gear I sensed something had changed after that night, and knew I would hurt deep down for the rest of my life. I had only hoped it wouldn't consume my wellbeing as it did my father.

Pacific North West

~

With Montana falling away behind me, I couldn't help but wonder how anything ahead on my travels was going to beat last night.

With my mind full of so many thoughts I tried to focus on one thing. I picked her to fill my thoughts.

Her smile so perfect, I saw us running in the rain, splashing through puddles, and huddling under awnings long enough to steal a kiss before running back out into the rain.

These thoughts made Idaho fly by quicker than I imagined. I crossed into Washington and immediately began to see so many things I had never seen before - the small shops, the little towns. I pulled over at a small diner to eat a nice hot meal. I wanted something to fill me up heartily, as I hadn't eaten much since the amusement park.

I sat down at a window side table to watch the local folks around town, when a voice brought me back to the diner.

"Can I get you something to drink?"

I turned to see a face of porcelain, eyes hazel – nearly green, long dark hair pulled back from her face, and the voice of an angel.

"Hey, can I get you something to drink?"

Embarrassed I replied "Water please, thank you."

She walked away and I was in disbelief. I hadn't looked at someone like that in a very long time. By the time she returned with my water I was ready to order.

"What can I get for you?"

"I'll have the pot roast and potatoes please, and can I ask you a question."

While she finished writing down my order she replied, "Sure thing."

"Could you tell me the best place to hike around here?"

She smiled ear to ear. "A hiker, are you? Well, you must try Okanogan-Wenatchee National Forest. By far the best besides Olympic National park but that's some ways away from here."

I smiled. "Thank you I'll try it out in the morning."

After consuming a meal that I couldn't get enough of and paid the check I heard a voice.

"Excuse me."

I turned to see what she wanted. "Yes?"

"You should start your hike at the third trail line - that's my favorite."

I smiled. "I just might do that, thank you."

That night I had a pocketful of bread from dinner and a bottle of water that would be my companions near the third trail line. I figured if someone went out of their way to tell me about a place they like, I may as well try it out.

~

I felt guilty that morning. I thought of the waitress from the night before, even though I didn't know her name. Nevertheless, I strapped on my boots and gear, tossed my pack over my back and departed the van.

After only a few steps I heard someone talking.

"Do you always take the advice of complete strangers?"

I turned to see the waitress from last night. "Do you always stalk your customers?"

She laughed. "I wanted to tell you my name, Cieana. I never got yours."

"I'm Jackson."

She approached "Well, I wanted to see if you'd show up. I hike here almost every morning, and cannot get enough. Do you mind if I join you?"

"No, absolutely not. I'll follow you, seeing this is your place."

Her smile made me smile as we headed off down her favorite trail. I couldn't believe she was taking such a risk heading out into the middle of nowhere with a complete stranger.

She turned to me "I cannot believe you're just going to follow a complete stranger in to the woods."

I laughed. "I was thinking the same thing about you."

"I figure life is an adventure, and I can read people very well. So less talking - let's get moving."

I followed her for about twenty minutes into a clearing that overlooked a beautiful ice capped glacier. I stood in amazement; in awe of how much beauty I have been missing out on my entire life. I turned to see her smiling; I could feel my face light up. "What?"

Pacific North West

Chapter Four

MIDDLE of NOWHERE

"You seem so much happier out here in the middle of nowhere than you did in the café last night."

I felt a rush come over me from the cool glacier air. "I would have never in a million years have expected to see this, let alone be given a tour by someone as nice as yourself."

She smiled "Are you trying to make me turn as red as you are?"

Her smile grew as I searched for a quick answer. "No…No the wind is really very cold on my sensitive skin."

She laughed at me, with a brilliant smile.

"Well if we're done embarrassing one another, I have much more to show you."

I followed her for the rest of the day. We hiked for miles and miles, overlooking some of the most beautiful landscapes, and backdrops I had ever seen. I wanted this day to continue forever, but the sun was beginning to set and we were almost back to my van.

"Well this was a fun day! I should get home to take care of my dog. My roommate let her out today but won't be back tonight."

Not knowing if I would ever see her again I replied "Have a good evening, thank you so much for the tour today. I had a lot of fun."

She zipped up her pack and loaded it into her car. "Not sure how long you'll be in town for, but tomorrow I'm working, and the day after I'll be hiking the beach down below here, if you're interested."

Attempting not to seem to overly excited I replied, "I'll be in town for a few more days, then I'm off to Olympic National Park, but I'd be happy to tag along."

"Okay, meet me on the second trail, it opens at nine AM and be ready to get cold and wet."

I nodded and smiled. While I watched her drive away I knew I had to find something more suitable than my van for the next couple of nights while I was in town.

~

I had only driven a couple of miles outside the park when I noticed log cabins set back off the road. I pulled in to see if there were any available for a couple of nights.

Upon entering the main lodging cabin, I was greeted by the sweetest little old lady.

"Hello dear, how may I help you?"

"I'm looking for a place to stay for the next couple of nights, and wanted to know if you had any available cabins."

The old woman smiled warmly. "That accent isn't from around here. I bet you're on some sort of adventure way out here. I have the perfect cabin for you. By the way, my name is Joyce Thomas."

She handed my keys to cabin "J", and in exchange I handed her money to pay for the room. "I'm Jackson Mathews. Pleased to meet you."

"Now take the road back to the end of the line and it's the cabin up the little hill, you're going to love the view."

I smiled as I exited the lodge. "Thank you again!"

A short drive down the road and a climb up the front steps of the cabin, I jiggled the key and pushed the door open, and couldn't believe what was in front of me.

The interior was beautiful light wood throughout with a sleeping loft above the back wall of the cabin that happened to be all glass, looking over the most amazing mountain view, a floor to ceiling fireplace made of stone, and some rustic furniture capped it off.

"All of this for such a nominal fee; I might have to stay a little bit longer."

I had myself all unpacked and ready for a night of good rest in a comfortable bed. With thoughts of the hike to come I was nervous and excited all at once. My heart raced with excitement, as I lay in the loft looking out into the night.

A mind full of thoughts that weren't my usual self-pity and despair. I had human interaction today that left me wanting more, and not making me want to turn and run for the hills.

~

That night went by in a hurry, I heard wolves howl. You want to talk about a crazy set of chills? I was in love with this place, all the wildlife, the most perfect cabin and the ability to see so many things I never knew existed.

As much as I wanted to go to the restaurant to see Cieana, I knew not to be the weird guy. Besides after tomorrow I would leave here and more than likely never see her again. After all, this place had much more to offer than strapping myself down with a single person the entire time I were here.

I also thought that she hadn't given me her number, nor did she offer it. May have slipped her mind, I haven't used my phone in days, other than as a flashlight.

While on my way out I stopped by the lodge to again thank Miss Thomas for such an amazing room.

"Hello, I wanted to thank you, that cabin is amazing!"

She smiled so sweetly. "I just knew you would love it. please let me know if you need anything during your stay."

"I will, absolutely, and thank you again."

My first journey for the day was to find food, and then I wanted to find a local bookstore to brush up on my surroundings. After all, my conversational skills aren't the best, and with not knowing much about the

Pacific North West

area I needed something to talk about when the air grew silent.

~

I found the most eclectic little bookstore at the bottom of a long twisting road, right in the middle of town. They served food in a small café, and you could read for free if you ate while in the store.

I read up on local vegetation, wildlife, and weather, and from what I read I should have been rained on almost the entire time I had been here.

I wasn't wishing my time in this place away, but I was ready to start tomorrow and get my first ever beach hike under way.

For some reason or another I felt secure in this strange and unusual place with so many friendly people and happy faces smiling at you all of the time. I guessed it would probably take a lifetime to find so many friendly strangers back home.

The night settled in fast upon me as I drifted off to sleep in the loft. I had slept more soundly than the night before, the most sleep I had gotten in a long while. I had begun to enjoy this place so very much. I had begun to enjoy life.

~

All morning I struggled with what I would say, or how I would greet her... if she showed up. Before I could park the van and get out, I saw her waiting for me at the beginning of the trail down to the beach.

"I started to think that you weren't going to show, that maybe you skipped town on me."

"No…No I had to at least see the beaches of the Pacific before I leave town."

Her grin and shake of her head were enough to tell me she didn't think I was as funny as I did.

"Well if it's the ocean you want to see it's that way, I mean I see it three to four times a week. I guess I'll head back home and catch up on my laundry."

I knew when I was beaten. "Well of course the beach wouldn't be anything special without a guide such as you."

"Uh huh, follow me please."

She smiled as she walked by. I couldn't help but smile thinking that there was a person in this world that made me forget about what I had lost for more than a minute.

"Well, there you are - the Pacific Ocean."

I looked up in awe at the waves crashing against the rocks, the sound of the water, and the beauty of the beach. It all highlighted the beauty of the one standing in front of me. I had been trying not to feel anything for her, because I knew nothing could come from this, and I was on my way out in the morning.

She smiled it seemed, just watching me smile.

"This is amazing! Would you mind if I take a few pictures before we move on?"

"Take your time." She murmured smiling.

Pacific North West

With every click of the camera I was building a collection of photographs that would one day remind me of what it felt like to be alive.

Chapter Five

QUESTIONS

Our hike began along a wide stretch of beach. I followed behind on another quiet hike. I began to wonder if she really wanted me with her, or that she really had no one else to hike with?

The beach gave way to a more unsteady, rocky terrain that was a bit slippery from the earlier morning rain. We hiked for a few miles in and up when we came to a clearing overlooking the ocean.

She stopped "This is one of the best views for photographing."

I moved closer to the edge and couldn't believe my eyes. I could feel myself smiling from the inside. "This is beautiful! Do you mind if I sit here for a while and take a few photos?"

She smiled "Not at all, that's why I brought you here."

era, while she set out a
ed up a hammock. This
ouldn't have done back
of freedom was
ght I had known before,
had I ever really been

I ask you a question or two:

She hopped up into her hammock "No, not at all."

I looked through the lens clicking away "You invite me out with you and yet we don't speak a word while we hike. Why?"

She sat up. "I keep quiet because I've seen most of the hikes around here, but I don't want you to miss the beauty of this place while talking."

Still I had more questions for her. "Why is it that you are you so trusting? I mean you have no idea who or what I am? Yet you follow or let me follow you into the middle of the woods, or up in the cliffs."

She hopped out of her hammock and walked right up against me.

"Have you ever just known you wanted something? I mean you really wanted something, and just had to take a chance on it? That's how I feel about you and have no idea why, but the feeling I get from you makes me feel alive in a place where I haven't been for so long."

I saw so many things in her face, without thinking I grabbed her and began to kiss her. I would have never done anything like this a few days ago.

After the kiss, she sat down upon the blanket, I joined her. "How couldn't you feel alive in a place as beautiful as this?"

She pulled at a flower she had picked from next to the blanket and placed it behind her ear.

"It is beautiful here, don't get me wrong, but when you've been here your entire life, have never left, and wait tables with not much ever going on besides the weekend hikers that want to jump your bones - If that's what you mean by a beautiful place, then yeah, this is it."

I wasn't expecting the answer she had given. In life you can never really judge someone or their situation accurately without knowing all of them.

"I would have never guessed that. Why haven't you ever traveled or just run away for a while?"

She lay back in on the blanket. "I've been held here, or at least I feel that way. My parents both died in a climbing accident when I was seventeen. My grandmother took me in, and when I turned eighteen I moved into my own place with my roommate. Since then I cope with what has become of my life. What about you, what brings you all the way out here?"

I normally would have never gotten into a personal conversation with someone I hardly knew. But there was something comforting about her.

"I had a rough upbringing. My mother passed away when I was a small boy. My father passed away shortly after I turned eighteen. I lost it one morning at work and hit my boss, quit my job and headed across country to find myself."

She laughed. "You hit your boss? Then just decided to drive across country. I can't even bring myself to leave this city. Why did you choose this part of the country? Usually people want to go to sun and palm trees."

I chuckled thinking of what I was about to say. "I started loading up my van and there it was, a flyer for a local band playing called "The Pacific North West. So, I took that as a sign, and here I am."

For a minute, she was silent, then began rolling back and forth laughing. "You drove all the way across the country because you read a flyer? That's the best thing I've heard in a very long time."

After hearing the story from someone else, it did sound a bit crazy.

"Okay now that we've had our fun, making fun of me, can we watch the sunset from higher up?"

"Help me pack up and I'll get you a good view of the sunset."

We packed up and hiked a few more miles to yet another beautiful clearing, a bluff overlooking the ocean. I was once again impressed by the beauty of the natural world.

"I have to let you know that I'm leaving here in the morning, and I'm not sure if I'll ever come back."

She exhaled deeply. "I know, and normally I wouldn't have let someone kiss me, especially someone I had just met. But I feel alive with you, I feel lightening in a bottle with you. I won't ever ask you to stay. I only wanted to know you."

I thought of home, of that cemetery that I have spent so much time in. I felt that if I had any feelings toward Cieana, that my feelings would be irrelevant for her.

"Thank you for everything."

We held one another in a beautiful sunset being chased away by rain clouds. I followed quietly behind her, back to the beach. We hugged and said our goodbyes.

We both knew there was no reason to make it harder than it was. We hugged, a short kiss goodbye, and went our separate ways.

~

Tears built behind her show of strength, "Why was it that life is and always will be so unfair? I find this perfect human that has chinks in his armor he's not afraid to show, and a heart deeper than I could explore. I know there won't be much sleep tonight."

Cieana was drained. Life had reared its head once more, taking something from her.

~

While the warm late spring air wrapped itself around me I couldn't help but think of the damage I caused to such a beautiful soul, and how un-deserving of this she was. With nothing more to do I figured I would stop in and talk to Miss. Thomas.

"Good evening, Jackson. How are you tonight?"

I'm not sure why but I sat in a porch swing across from her. I hadn't planned on staying long, just enough to say goodbye and thank her for her kindness.

"Good evening, Miss. Thomas, I stopped in this evening to say goodbye, and to thank you for your hospitality. I'll be leaving in the morning."

She was silent for a minute as she stared at me.

"I must have been wrong, I guess. I figured you would want to stay here for a little while longer."

Looking at her looking at me, it seemed as if she knew something, as if she could read me without me saying a word.

"What is it that you mean by that?"

She smiled.

We talked for more than an hour that night, I would never forget that conversation, and after all it would end up changing my life forever.

~

In full stride Cieana ran, her feet pounding against the ground, heart racing with every step that brought her closer to the cabins. "How could I just let him walk away without trying to get him to stay?"

She ran as fast as she could, knowing it was probably all but too late. She ran up the front steps of the main lodge, almost running into Miss. Thomas.

"I'm sorry to barge in here like this but have you seen a young man, his name is Jackson?"

"Of course, such a sweet young man, he was staying in the canyon lodge in the back of the park, but…"

Before she finished Cieana began running to the lodge, pushed the door open to an empty cabin and yelled out. "Jackson…Jackson."

She knew she had waited too long and that he was gone.

Without her knowing I had walked up behind her carrying a load of wood in my arms.

"Can I help you, young lady?"

She turned and charged me, knocking the wood from my arms and hugging me tighter than I've been hugged in a long while.

"How are you still here, I thought I was going to be too late, and I don't want you to leave. Not yet."

I had a feeling she would come here, at least I hoped she would.

"Last night I could think of nothing else but you. I wasn't ready to leave. I stopped in to talk to Mrs. Thomas, and, she asked me what was troubling me, so I explained to her about my time here, about you. That's when she asked me if I wanted to stay free all summer, and make some money working here. Keeping the wood chopped and the grounds clean, and if I did I could keep my cabin all summer. I had to accept."

Her face lit up the way I could imagine mine does at the sight of all my new surroundings.

"So, I have the entire summer with you?"

I laughed. "Wait, I said I'll be working here, not that we're hanging out together."

She pushed me. "Fine, then you can get lost in the woods all alone and eaten by something."

I laughed. She helped me pick up the wood and drop it off in front of the cabins for the campers evening fires.

"I have to get to work. I get out at seven and I was wondering if you'd like to hang out."

The way she smiled when she asked, as she moved her hand nervously was amazing.

"Of course, I would. Meet here at eight?"

Her response was sweeter than summer lavender.

"I'll see you then."

I couldn't believe the feelings that resonated inside of me. I was feeling down about them and at the same time I was almost happy.

My new job of cleaning up out in nature, splitting wood, taking care of cabins in the woods, the change of pace from that rat race I left behind was exhilarating.

How could I have been so lucky to find this place, to take this adventure? Then from my back pocket I pulled out my wallet and pulled out that wrinkled flyer for the "Pacific North West" concert. I kept it, not sure why, but I did know one thing, if it wasn't for this flyer, who knows where I would be right now.

Pacific North West

Chapter Six

BACKDROPS

Pacific North West

I had the impression after finishing my day of work that Miss Thomas knew what she was doing when she offered me the job here. The work itself was demanding, but physically rewarding at the same time. Having some time to burn I headed out back to the lake to sit and snap a few photos of the clouds rolling past.

The backdrops that nature painted out here were amazing, the blues, grays, purples, reds as if it were out of an artist's mind. I continued snapping away, thinking about home, or the place I used to call home, not sure if I would ever really leave that place behind completely, or if I was ready to at this point. I packed up my gear to get ready for Cieana's visit tonight.

~

She had planned everything we had done so far, so I took it upon myself to plan the night ahead.

I prepared a mixed green salad, along with spicy rice, loaded up the picnic basket and rushed out to the lake behind my cabin. I laid out the blanket, placed the basket, and built the teepee in the fire pit. "Not bad Jackson". I had one more task of strapping up my hammock between two of the log pillars on the front porch of my cabin, then headed inside for a well-deserved shower.

After my shower, I had a few minutes to relax and gather my thoughts. I waited for her on the front porch of my cabin, swinging in the hammock.

~

"Well, would you look at that, a slacker sleeping on his first day on the job?"

I leapt out of the hammock with a smile on my face. She looked amazing, dressed in light blue jeans ripped randomly in the front, a black tank top, and her hair braided down her back. Her green eyes gleamed, I couldn't believe I was falling for her, with no ability to stop it. Not sure if I wanted to even if I could.

"You look really nice."

She smiled. "Thank you, you're not so bad yourself. So, what do you want to do tonight?"

I picked my pack up from the porch. "Well, seeing that you've planned everything so far and I don't know my way around here all that well, I picked something close for us to do. Follow me."

Her face lit up as she followed me back around the cabins to a lake view, where I had the fire ready to be lit and a picnic dinner set out for us. Her face was enough to make me smile, just watching her smile.

"You did all of this for me?"

"I did. This way we don't have to rush in or out of somewhere, and we can stay here as long as we please."

We shared the green mix salad and the spicy rice I had prepared earlier while watching the fire dance. The flickering of the fire was breathtaking, but that night the fire flies that stole the show. They danced across a cloudy backdrop, which had been every shade of gray, fighting to keep the moon hidden from sight.

With dinner finished we had time to sit and talk, to enjoy one another's company, or so we thought. The clouds began to open, and a downpour broke loose. Soaking wet, we picked up our belongings and raced for the cover of my cabin's front porch.

"Well, I guess this is goodnight. I had a very nice time with you. Thank you for being so thoughtful."

I wasn't ready to let her go. I wasn't sure if I was ever going to be ready, but for now I knew I could keep her.

"You don't have to leave, you're more than welcome to come in and stay a while."

I could see that she wanted to, but didn't want to seem too eager.

"I'm not sure, it's getting pretty late and I should be going home."

Before she could say another word, I took her by the hand.

"Please stay for a little while."

With both of us soaking wet we entered the cabin, I led her to an enormous rug that lay in front of the fireplace. She watched me as I started a fire to help dry us out.

I remember turning to see the fire flickering in her eyes of green. I was lost, there was no coming back from this, she had me and I didn't care.

~

We began talking, that night we talked about anything and everything. She could get me to talk about things I had sworn to silence.

"You said you hit your boss and drove across country. There must be something that was pushing you, some sort of a driving force."

Pacific North West

I thought about her question for a moment before answering.

"I have never talked about it with anyone, and I'm not sure how it will go talking about it with you, but here goes. I found an angel on earth. We shared so many similar interests. We were inseparable, until one night I received a phone call. She had been hit by a drunk driver while crossing the street, only three blocks from home. My life ended as I knew it that night, when she was killed instantly by the impact. After that I decided I had to leave that place and try to live again."

Tears rolled down the side of her face, she held my hand as we sat gazing into the fire.

"I'm so sorry. I didn't mean to pry. I only want to get to know you. I had no idea."

I didn't want her to feel bad about my opening up to her.

"No...No you did nothing wrong. I wanted to tell you about her. She has been the driving force behind me for some time now, and when I met you something changed. I thought there would be no way I could ever feel like this about someone ever again. I felt guilty at first, but I know she would want me happy, and something steered me all the way to you."

A brief silence fell over the room before she replied.

"So, you feel a certain way about me?"

Her smile broke the mood in the room.

"I do."

I held her in front of the fire, knowing this was something else in life that could cause me pain. I felt so out of control in that moment that I wasn't sure of what I had done. All I knew was holding her felt like home.

I had always felt that home wasn't a place. Home was the way the people you were with made you feel.

She started to fall asleep.

"Do you need to get home or can you stay?"

She stretched. "I can stay if you don't mind."

"I would like that. You can sleep up in the loft, I'll stay down here."

She laid back into my arms.

"Can you hold me for a while, and stay right here?"

I was more than happy to do so. "Of course."

The fire danced as she slept in my arms, I watched her breath and had a feeling there was more to her story than I knew.

She was so soundly sleeping in my arms and yet we barely knew one another. I had a feeling she felt safe with me, as I did with her.

~

When I woke up the following morning she was gone. A note on the kitchen table read "You looked so peaceful I didn't want to wake you. Thank you for letting me sleep in your arms. I have to get to work. I'll be out around five this evening if you want to hang out."

I smiled, and then I laughed. Why hadn't we exchanged phone numbers yet? But I guess we haven't even needed to call one another yet.

I had to get to work anyway, chopping, delivering wood, cleaning up campsites, and the grounds from all the vacationers that would leave more than their footprint behind.

I stopped into the lodge and sat a while with Miss Thomas.

"How are you today?"

She sat in her rocking chair.

"I'm holding up. Sure am glad you decided to stay. I think you'll love this place, and all the surroundings. Besides it looks like you're making friends as well."

She smiled at me.

"I'm glad as well. This place is incredible. As far as friends, she is something out of a story book. I mean, I cannot begin to explain how she makes me feel."

Miss Thomas smiled. "I have been in this town for some years now and everyone here has a story. You should try and get her to tell you hers. I promise you this. You'll understand why I think you should."

"I will. Thank you."

Chapter Seven

A HURTFUL REMINDER

I wasn't sure of the relationship I found myself in with Pierce, people around me thought it made sense, but I wasn't sure of the inner dynamics of the disaster I called life. Did my coworkers and friends think I was lucky to be with him because he was rich? Did I see it as a disaster as I became aware of his dark side?

Life in a small town held a few guarantees - the same old people, and little to no way out unless you simply ran away.

With my parents gone at an early age I found myself in search of acceptance and one sure way to get it was from Pierce, a local rich kid that had all of daddy's money he could ever spend.

He was picture perfect with his dusty blonde hair, blue eyes and a face chiseled to perfection. At first I wasn't sure if it was his new Escalade, small palace he called his winter home decked out with an in ground pool, hot tub and more than enough stereo equipment to fill a theater.

Or maybe it was his kind and generous side that appealed to me at first. The amount of thought and time he put into capturing my heart from the beginning. From the candle lit dinners to the late night strolls on the beach. He had won my heart and for a while my heart turned a blind eye to what had turned into a nightmare of a life.

Don't get me wrong the beginning was good, I thought I loved him.

To say our relationship was volatile was an understatement. The fighting intensified as I began to drift away from him. My Grandmother never approved the relationship; she had seen my bruises on my arms when he grabbed me a little too tight, my heartbreak and hurt caused by his controlling behavior, the constant insults and criticism of my life.

After the first time he hit me I blamed the drinking that night, I guess after the third or fourth time flowers, jewelry and apologies kept me hoping that he was going to change.

"I have to work late tonight Pierce, so I won't make it to the party at your place."

He hated when I worked late or didn't show up to an event at his home. He thought I was cheating or up to something. You need to worry more about someone like that than they do about you.

"Why are you still working at that crappy diner? I told you, no girl of mine is going to work in a place like that. Besides there are too many random guys from out of town passing through that place."

I felt smaller and smaller inside every time he belittled me, though I wanted to be loved so badly, but that night I had enough.

He grabbed me hard by my arms and began to shake me, which was relatively benign treatment compared to the pushing, hitting, yelling.

Pacific North West

"Listen to me, you know you're nothing without me and you *will* always be nothing!"

I tried to pull away from him and he slapped me in the face. I was stunned but kneed him straight in the groin and ran for the door. I knew he would chase me, so I ran straight to the diner to begin my shift.

My days after that incident were plagued with this behavior. Was this the final break up and or would he continue harassing me to get back together again? My only saving grace was summer was on the horizon and he left every summer to live it up, or "work" as he called it, at his father's private retreat in the Barbados.

I looked at myself in the bathroom mirror of the diner and decide to change my life and find myself out in the wild. I took up hiking, backpacking, and the love of nature. I adopted a beautiful four legged friend and she became the love of my life, plus she was my new protector.

Belle appeared a much scarier dog than she was, but she wouldn't let people to close to me unless I let her know they were a friend. In a way, she saved me and kept Pierce at a distance, as he was terrified of big dogs. Figures someone as tough as him feared a creature so sweet. Would my life ever be normal? I wasn't sure what normal was anymore. I knew what I wanted in life, and knew when I found it I wouldn't let it get away.

Most people wait for great things to happen in life, but in my experience, waiting only causes life to become stale and leaves you wanting things you should be running after.

~

I had a firm awareness at this point that I had no idea what life would bring; the ever-surprising ideas that will jump up and shake you awake at any moment, during any day.

Pacific North West

I had some time left before Cieana would be finished working, so I wandered the local artisan market.

Amazed by the works of art people could create with their own two hands, I knew exactly what I had been looking for as soon as I saw it.

"How much for the sunflowers?"

The cart owner replied "Seven dollars."

I picked up a bouquet and handed the man seven dollars. "Thank you, have a good day."

Now armed with flowers in hopes that I wouldn't embarrass her at her work I began in that direction.

Figuring that the park bench just across the two-lane road would be a beneficial vantage point, I sat in wait.

My face lit up as she exited the diner. "Cieana, over here."

She smiled when she looked up and ran across the street. "What are you doing here?"

"Well, I finished up with work, went for a walk and now I'm here. Oh and these are for you."

She held them close to her face and inhaled. "I absolutely love sun flowers. Thank you so much!"

She followed with a big hug. "I have to go home and take care of my puppy. Do you mind coming with me?"

"Not at all, we should bring her out with us tonight. I mean if you want to."

Hand in hand we walked to her apartment only a few blocks down the street.

"That would be awesome, she would love to get out, and I feel as if I have been neglecting her."

~

Tree lined roads eventually gave way to forest, streams, waterfalls and wildlife of all sizes, so many incredible sights, and that was a normal walk home to her apartment.

"Should I wait here?" I asked to be polite.

"No...No, come on in. Bella may jump on you. She loves people."

As soon as I entered the house I was pounced on by a beautiful terrier that was attempting to lick me to death.

"Bella, sit! Good girl. I'm going to clean up really quick and then we can head out."

The apartment smelled of lavender and citrus, and a light airy vibe flowed throughout the home. I sat waiting on the living room couch with Bella licking my hand.

"You're a good girl, aren't you? Do you want to hang out with us tonight, pretty girl?"

Not knowing I was being watched, I heard Cieana.

"Looks like I have some competition."

Bella ran to her and sat ready to go for her walk. Cieana wrapped a harness around Bella and a leash to her harness. We were ready to go.

"I guess I haven't thought about it. What would you like to do tonight?"

"Well, seeing we have my big baby, we're more limited. Maybe ice cream in town and a walk on the beach?"

Ice cream did sound delicious. "That sounds perfect. Lead the way."

~

Bella, very well behaved, followed close at Cieana's side. Smells of sugar and food began to fill the air, the closer we approached into town. Looking at a busy night here in this town as opposed to where I had left, the difference was amazing.

Here I could handle busy, much more my speed. I could hear individuals conversing, sounds more soothing than yelling and honking horns at someone for a second of delay.

"I have been watching you this entire time and your face is priceless. You've come from such a big city and yet this little town continues to impress you."

She caught me red handed. "I understand opposite ends of the spectrum now. This place is so full of life, when where I come from is just so full of life in a different way. There are life forms where I come from, but most people seem so beaten down and lifeless. Out here everyone has so much going on, and more than just a work and home kind of life."

She smiled as we sat at an outside table to order our ice cream.

We ordered vanilla sundaes and a doggy cup for Bella. My life had turned into a dream. How have I gotten so lucky after all this suffering? I would never know.

That night we talked for hours about everything and nothing at all, I could feel her getting closer to me. I didn't want to ask about her entire story just yet.

"So, what would a normal night consist of for you after working all day, had I not been around?"

She paused for a moment.

"Well, when I actually stop and think about it, I guess it's really pretty sad. I would walk home, clean up, change into something comfortable and hang out with this fur baby right here."

"In my world that would be nothing but a good time back home. I was never comfortable there, at least not in recent history. If you think about it, the way that our two worlds have collided is really quite amazing."

She smiled "What do you mean?"

"Two people, both not exactly happy in their own life, meeting by chance, having everything and nothing in common all at the same time. They take a risk on one another and begin to develop this snowball of a relationship, kind of miraculous."

The way she looked at me after my previous statement left me wondering what she was thinking until she spoke.

"This really is kind of miraculous. I know life has always existed and so much has happened in both of our lives, but the thought of you not with me is kind of non-existent."

I felt as if I knew what she was aiming for but I had to ask.

"What do you mean?"

She rested against the back of her chair.

"I mean I know we both have lives, and had lives before this summer and I'm not sure if this is coming out right but, I feel as if life didn't exist before you. I know it did, but now it feels like life is worth more than a day to day walk through life."

I took a minute to take in what she had said.

"I feel similarly. I mean I too feel like life is better now, almost easier with you. The simple thought of you in my head can distract me like a dog chasing a squirrel. I know my past is there waiting to surprise me at any minute, but you make that thought not as terrifying as it used to be. I know for sure I no longer want to walk this life without you."

Worried if that may have been too much for her to handle, I waited for a response.

"You don't have too. I'm here for you now."

~

Our walk back to her apartment entailed hilly back roads, chirping night creatures and the sounds of people enjoying life. Upon arriving at her front steps, she leaned in close to me. We hugged and kissed goodnight.

"Are you sure you don't want to stay here tonight?"

I wanted to more than anything. I didn't want to be away from her.

 "I have to get up really early and split a bunch of wood. The grounds are all booked for the entire weekend. Will I see you tomorrow?"

She smiled. "I have the day off tomorrow, so if you would like some company and or help I'll be over by nine."

This was music to my ears. "I would like that very much. I'll see you then."

She closed the door behind her with a smile upon her face. She knew she had fallen and fallen hard. She would sleep well tonight; her life had transformed into a story book over a short time this summer.

~

I felt amazing; my body felt weightless as I walked home, thinking more and more of my days ahead, and much less of days past. If life were lived more in the present and focused on the future, rather than living in the past and dwelling I believe everyone would be much happier. Not to say forget your entire existence up to the point of today. The scars are there to remind us, but they don't have to control us, or our destiny.

Pacific North West

Chapter Eight

NIGHTMARES

That night a nightmare woke me from an unusually deep sleep in the loft. I heard the phone ringing, when I answered it that night replayed.

"Is this Jackson Mathews?"

"Yes. Who is this?" I asked.

"Sir this is Bi County Hospital, your fiancée, Michelle, has been in an accident."

I couldn't believe I was hearing this again. "What do you mean an accident, she doesn't drive? Is she okay, is she alive?"

"I'm so sorry sir. She has passed away."

Tears immediately fell to the ground. I went to go identify her at the hospital. I saw her lying there with bloodstains in her clothes and hair. I walked from the hospital and considered the road. I wanted to step in front of the first bus that passed.

In the next few days I would plan her burial. Neither of us had any family, so I stood in watch as they put her to rest.

Weeks of torture ensued as I sat watching the trial of the man that hit her. He was convicted on involuntary manslaughter, sentenced to ten years in jail without parole.

He gets ten years, while she is in the ground forever, to me it never made sense, nor will it.

There would be no going back to sleep tonight. I sat looking out into the wild, watching an occasional shadow move about, and the comforting howls from the local wolf pack.

Nightmares that were unfortunately just a rendering of my life made it near impossible for me to let my guard down. Feelings I have inside of me are beginning to grow for someone new. I hoped these nightmares weren't a reminder of my past bent on keeping me there.

~

Sunrise was a welcome sight. I could finally get to work. Starting at this hour I should be done before noon. Miss Thomas was far too kind with her offer, she tries to pay me on top of giving me minimal work.

With every swing of the axe the night before drifted out of mind. My new concern was if I were to stay here, if something real happened between Cieana and myself, would I be able to give her my all, knowing how my past still affects me?

"Hey you, how are you this morning?"

My smile reappeared to the sound of her voice.

"Better now! I have another three hours or so here and then we're free for the day."

She picked up a log and tossed it in the barrow. "Well enough talking, let's get to work."

Her ability to make the best out of every situation was amazing. I watched her work while I split log after log, I couldn't help but stare at her.

Hours flew by and the grounds were clean and fully stocked. By now the days were in the mid-eighties, and I was ready to jump in a cold lake.

We stood at the back of my cabin when I kicked off my boots and sock pulled my shirt off and ran for the water.

"Last one in cooks dinner!"

She pulled her shoes off and gave chase in her tank top and jeans.

We both hit the water at the same time. She was faster than I thought.

"How did you catch me so fast?"

With a grin, she splashed me. "See, when your naturally faster than your opponent, it's easy to catch them."

"Oh...I see how it is."

I picked her up and splashed under water with her, we resurfaced holding one another. We kissed, I'm not sure how long, but I knew one thing - it wasn't long enough.

We chased one another splashing from the lake "I'll build a fire for us to dry out by?"

"That would be great."

Having a warm fire after a swim in the not so warm lake was great. We sat. I had to ask this time.

"So, what is your story? Why are you single out here? To me it seems you could probably have anyone that you wanted."

She smiled softly.

"I live a single life to keep from being hurt, disappointed, neglected, abused, all of the above. My ex wasn't the kindest soul. He would yell, swear, and even hit me. I figured once I freed myself of him and he moved away I would stay alone, that way I wouldn't get hurt anymore. I would be safe in my loneliness."

I felt terrible.

"I'm so sorry, I would have never asked if..."

Before I could finish she interjected.

"No... No, I wanted to tell you I just didn't want to dampen any of our time together, it's been so nice. Besides I'm sure my grandmother put you up to asking anyways."

In shock, I looked at her.

"Miss Thomas is your grandmother? That explains a lot."

Cieana sat up from the grass. "Explains what?"

"That night I had gone to say goodbye to her she offered me the job and to stay the summer. She knew we had been hanging out."

She smiled.

"She also knew how happy you were making me. My grandmother is all the family I have left. She wants you to know my past, because she thinks we can help one another heal."

I stood from my seated position.

"Well, knowing that I think we have some solid ground to stand upon."

She stood.

"I know that this has been fun and I also know you're only here through the season. But I don't want you to go."

I wasn't sure of what to say.

"I haven't thought that far ahead; I have no real home. This place sure feels like home, and you, I know I don't want to be without you. I'm not sure what that means or how you want to take it, but it's all that I have right now."

She smiled. "Well for now let's enjoy one another and not think too far ahead."

We watched the lake side by side for the next couple of hours; the fish jumping was a nice distraction. I wanted to be with her, but wanted to protect myself from being hurt at the same time.

We had been pulled into one another so quickly that I waited for it to evaporate in the same manor.

Would I be here after the end of summer; could I take her somewhere with me? Only time would tell, and that was something I was willing to wait and see.

"Would you like to head in and make some dinner?"

"What do you mean make some dinner? I beat you to that water, your cooking, slow poke."

I helped her from the grass and entered the cabin from the door wall, to prepare dinner.

~

I prepared chicken for the grill to put overtop of rice, with a summer salad on the side. Since my arrival here it seems like I had been eating much healthier food, and that it was kind of way of life around here.

I looked over and noticed she had fallen asleep on the couch. I watched her sleep for some time not wanting to wake her.

Could it be that this is where I belong; did I even need to go any further in my journey? I hoped that this was the real thing. I kept expecting to wake up from a dream, back to my old life of suffering.

I had more time than originally thought, so I set the table and lit candles before I woke her.

"Hey beautiful, wake up. Dinners ready."

She woke up and was amazed, almost brought to tears. "You did all of this for me?"

I could see she was moved by my dinner setting. I hugged her and walked her to the table, and we sat across from one another talking into the night.

"I feel like the lifestyle here is a way healthier one than that back home."

She laughed.

"With all of the outdoor activity here this time of year people generally try to be more conscientious about their habits. But in the winter all bets are off, the local shops make some of the best comfort foods around. Deserts, stews, smoked everything. You'll see."

I figured I would see the winter here. I no longer had any desire to be any place else, no reason to go on any further in my journey. My journey was to the Pacific Northwest and here I was.

"I can't wait to see winter here."

Her smile let me know she understood I would be staying.

"Besides the light festival in the winter is almost as amazing as the harvest festival in the fall, I cannot wait to show it all to you."

The feeling of excitement about events and times to look forward to made me happy, a feeling that had been too long absent from my life.

~

After dinner, we cleaned up together.

"Would you like to stay tonight?"

She nodded. "Yes...Yes I would."

She hugged me then we began to kiss. We made our way to the loft and undressed one another. The closeness of our bodies was exhilarating, feeling her pressed against me. She pulled me closer her, the night shone through the glass surrounding the loft. We were in a storm of ourselves that I had no desire to ever end.

~

We sat holding one another, neither tired of gazing out into the night sky, painted all but perfectly. I wanted to say something, anything but the words that wanted to come out weren't going to be right. When I figured out something to say she had broken the silence.

"That was incredible, and I know you're going to run for the hills when I tell you this but, I'm falling hard for you. I want to keep myself protected but at the same time I want to be open for you, for this."

My mind raced as I searched for a response, when I realized that if I just open my mouth the right words will come out. After all, I felt the same way.

"You're the first person that I've been able to have feelings about in a very long time. I know that opening up could lead to heart break and believe me, I wanted to run for a second. After spending time with you, I knew I would fall harder for you than I could have ever imagined. You have made my life worth getting up for, my life has purpose, and I will do everything in my being to keep you safe. I ask that you protect my heart because it now beats for you."

Her face was still with the moonlight shining off her, she was so beautiful.

"I would never hurt you. I need you in my life. Ever since you arrived in the spring my days have been filled with happiness. Please know that I will be here for you no matter what."

I laughed. "Funny thing you say that."

She knew I was up to something. "What is it?"

"I want you to take me cliff diving, I've seen so many doing it since I've been here, and it looks awesome."

Now her face lit up.

"I would love to take you. It's so much fun and what a rush. I know the perfect spot, we can go tomorrow, but I must bring Bella. She loves the cliffs. She won't dive but loves running up and down them."

"That sounds perfect."

We watched the night sky while listening to the howling pack of wolves. She was first to fall asleep, as I held her in my arms I couldn't help but think of how lucky I was to stop here and eat in that diner.

I haven't felt warmth like this in what seems like forever, and with the comfort of her body next to mine, I was going to sleep like a log tonight.

Pacific North West

Pacific North West

Chapter Nine

HOME

Cieana ran with Bella in pursuit until she disappeared over the cliffs edge. I was just behind her, as I jumped over the edge. Cieana splashed seconds before me. When I hit the water a jolt went through me. What an amazing feeling to be free, just falling into a safety net of water.

"Wow! What a rush, I cannot believe how much fun that is."

She smiled at me as if she knew I was going to enjoy myself.

"I wasn't sure if you were going to go through with it or not. When people get close to the edge they tend to pull back and not leap."

I wanted to jump again as quickly as possible. "I have to go once more."

Her smile was an ever-amazing sight.

"You go ahead, I'm going to build a small fire on the beach and get the blankets laid out."

I walked up the Cliffside passing a charging Bella eager to see Cieana. The beauty of everyday life was incredible. I was about to jump over a cliff and spend the rest of the afternoon on a secluded beach with a beautiful person. I had left the east in search of life, only to find out I was the reason I wasn't living at all.

I looked over the edge before I jumped this time, thinking about all the things I needed to let go of, and maybe jumping over the edge will signify a new life for me, a change in my world.

Free falling with no fear of falling is an incredible thing. I felt weightless, to be so free if only for a few seconds nonetheless, free was a feeling I was all too unfamiliar with.

~

The water brisk, the scenery picturesque and the beauty that is Cieana sat by the flickering fire waiting for my return for lunch.

"How was the second jump?"

I smiled more and more every time I heard her voice.

"Life changing!"

As if she knew what I thinking she said, "I cannot believe how fast this summer is racing by. The days keep getting shorter, as if they weren't short enough already."

I hadn't thought much about the time going by, or how fast it was truly going. I guess when life is a vacation you never want to focus on anything negative.

"I don't pay much mind to it really. I try not to cause myself any undue stress."

That day we sat simply holding one another while Bella slept on the foot of our blanket. Day leaned into night; sunset had to be one of the most beautiful sights I'd ever seen.

After having the thought of Fall on my mind I could feel crispness in the air. My time here had gone by so quickly and with no sense of urgency I hadn't at all prepared for the end of this beautiful mess I had entrenched myself in.

~

Along with my usual duties around the grounds, cleanup had become more and more taxing with all the added fall debris. Over the last couple of weeks, I felt Cieana starting to distance herself from me. She had been working more and not coming by every morning. She was trying to put off the inevitable or so I had thought.

I had finished up my work early that night and wanted to surprise her with a fire lit dinner, and a night under the stars before colder weather settles in.

I made my way up the hill to see Cieana holding onto another man as if she hadn't seen him in a while.

"So, this is why you haven't been around as much?"

She fumbled over her words, and then he spoke.

"I'm Pierce her boyfriend. I leave for the summer every year to help overseas. She hasn't mentioned me?"

I held back my anger. "It must have slipped her mind. I see you didn't need me, you wanted me. You two have a good night."

The walk back to the cabin was a little colder, and I wasn't exactly sure of anything, as if a wound was pulled open and my mind wouldn't stop racing.

I packed my bags and loaded up the van to head back east. Turns out you can get your heart broken in any part of the country and if I was broken, I wanted to be close to home, or at least a place that was familiar.

I dropped my keys and a letter to Miss Thomas on her desk and made tracks back east.

"I know you're in there. Open up this isn't funny Jackson."

Cieana pounded upon the cabin door to no avail, when she heard the voice of her grandmother from behind her.

"He has gone, my girl. He left a letter and his keys he said he was going back east."

She began to cry. "May I read the letter?"

Her grandmother handed the letter to her, she read it quietly.

"Miss Thomas, I didn't have it in me to talk on my way out, but I wanted to thank you for all of your hospitality. You gave a young outsider a chance and for that I'm grateful. I'm not sure what I'm going to do next but, I do know I'm heading back east to visit a few people before the snow hits, and then who knows maybe head down south. Anyways, thank you from the bottom of my heart for all that you did for me this summer. Signed, Sincerely Jackson."

She handed the letter back to her grandmother. "I'm going home, good night, Grandma."

Pacific North West

Chapter Ten

LIFE

Pacific North West

My drive back east was lackluster compared to my triumphant ride to the west. I wasn't sure why I was even going back at all. I have no family and very few people who would want to see me. In the back of my mind I knew exactly where I would end up. That old cemetery talking to the air, as I've done for years now, not sure of what to say anymore. I knew she would always listen.

I pulled into Jersey City late on a Thursday. The cemetery was closed and I was more than tired. I figured I should sleep, but hadn't the energy to find a place, so a cold van in a parking lot would have to do for the night.

~

My breath was visible due to a cold October morning; a cold rain fell as I stood in front of that grave that I had stood in front of so many times.

"Hello, I don't really know what to say anymore, I'm sorry that you were more distant in my thoughts this past summer. I have no idea what I was thinking. You were the only person that never hurt me that never let me down. I...I."

There was nothing left to say, I hit my knees and couldn't help but letting all the tears fall that I'd been holding back for so long. The feeling of being alone in this world began to wrap itself around me once again.

Lost in the moment or maybe just lost in time, my brain began to slow. I had yet to figure out what life was for, and why was it full of so much pain.

Pacific North West

The demons began to wrap themselves around me again; I had no control and was going down in a hurry, when I felt something strange on my face. I looked up.

"Bella, what are you doing here girl?"

Then from behind me I heard a shaky voice.

"You never gave me a chance to explain."

I wiped my face and walked from the cemetery. This was my own place.

"I didn't want to hear it back in Oregon, and I don't care to hear it now."

She wasn't going to leave without me hearing what she had to say.

"That guy, he came up and hugged me. Sure, he used to be my boyfriend but he hasn't been for a long time. He was horrible to me, and he goes to his father's private island for the summer to get away from the family business."

I stopped walking and turned around.

"Why were you so different at the end of summer?"

She wiped her face. "I didn't want to lose you, and I knew you were leaving soon."

I never understood why people would create distance from something that they soon wouldn't have. I lost people time after time and would never go back and distance myself from them.

"Go home, I'm done getting hurt."

She grabbed me and held on with a giant hug.

"No...No please I don't want to lose you. I love you! I'm so sorry. I don't just want you. I need you! Please don't walk away from me."

I didn't want to walk away but I didn't want to be hurt anymore. My life was a roller coaster of pain, some days more painful than others, but nonetheless pain every day. I hugged her back, after all if anyone could take my focus off my old life and make me whole again it was her.

"I love you too. I want life to be easier, I know what we had this summer and I want that every day. You made me whole again. I don't want to be empty anymore."

She wiped her eyes.

Will you come back west with me?"

I knew I was going west, but first there were a few things I wanted to show her.

"I'll make a deal with you. We'll head back west if we do it my way."

"And what would that be?" She asked.

Our journey back would duplicate the way I had traveled out west initially. I knew she had wanted to see life outside of the town she lived in, so I figured that was the least I could do, considering she had done so much to show me life in her world.

~

Our first stop would be Cedar Point. I couldn't wait to see her face after a roller coaster ride.

"That was incredible! How would anyone not enjoy this place?"

I took joy in watching her enjoy herself.

"Believe it or not most people will never see places like this no matter where they hail from. Take me for example, I had only read about this place or seen commercials for it on television. It took a life changing road trip to get to this place and see what it was all about."

"I cannot wait to see what else our journey back will hold!"

Side by side in my van we entered Chicago, I had the car transported back home, and as Bella was a service animal she was allowed where most dogs weren't. I had to show her The Field Museum as well as the Shedd Aquarium, then on to driving straight through back west.

~

"Thank you for taking me to these amazing places. I would have never even known most of them existed if we hadn't gone."

I was happy I could show her new things she found exciting.

"I'm so happy to see you smile about things that you haven't seen before. That's how you made me feel this entire summer."

We arrived in the early evening back to the lodge where I had worked all summer.

"Do you think your Grandmother has room in her heart to let me keep my cabin for the winter if I keep up the grounds?"

"Not sure. Why don't you turn around and ask her?"

I turned to see Miss Thomas standing on her porch.

"Young man, my intentions were to have you never leave. Your love for this place and the outdoors has restored my love for this place. See I hadn't been much in love with this place ever since the passing of my husband, her Grandfather. We opened this place together many years ago, and when I watched you two this summer it renewed my love for this place. You two reminded me of us all those years ago, two young kids with nothing more than a dream. But to answer your question, I wouldn't mind having someone else living on the grounds with me this winter. Besides I'll get to spend more time with my granddaughter."

I felt alive, I felt home.

"Thank you for all that you've done and continue to do for me. How about I run into town and gather some things for dinner and cook us a meal tonight? We can all eat and spend a nice evening together."

They looked at one another and smiled. Miss Thomas answered.

"That would be wonderful, my boy."

~

I had two bags of groceries, one in each arm, as I walked back to the steps of Miss Thomas's lodge. I couldn't help but feel something following me then I felt a pain as I was knocked to the ground.

I hurried to my feet turning to see Pierce standing in front of me.

"Do you really think you can make her happy? I have more money than a casino and couldn't keep her happy. She's mine and always will be mine. If I must I'll beat you like I did her."

I had heard enough and could tell his belligerence was more to do with the alcohol on his breath than his pompous courage.

I swung and hit him square in the mouth, something I had gotten good at as of late. He fell to the ground. I pounced on top of him and began to swing wildly, hitting him again and again. I heard a voice from behind yell out.

"Jackson stop, he's not worth it."

I stood and turned to see Cieana and Miss Thomas waiting for my return on the porch.

"Just let him go on his pathetic way to try and buy someone else."

I picked up my bags and looked at Pierce as he walked away ashamed.

"I'm back with the groceries, sorry you had to witness that. He jumped me from behind and said some things. I couldn't do the right thing this time."

Miss Thomas patted me on the shoulder.

"Oh, my boy you did the right thing, trust me."

I cooked a barley stew and had fresh bread bowls baking in the oven. Tonight we would eat heartily, and tonight we would celebrate life.

As I cooked I watched with a smile on my face as Cieana and her Grandmother engaged in conversation. When people say our journeys are laid out in a pattern, I couldn't help but believe in that now. Not only had my faith in life and humans been restored, I had helped restore life and that same belief in others this summer. I had brought a family closer to where they started rather than further from home!

Pacific North West

After all home isn't a place at all; its how the people in that place make you feel. For me home could be right here, or in my van, if I have these people here with me, my life would be lived at HOME!

Pacific North West